5/20

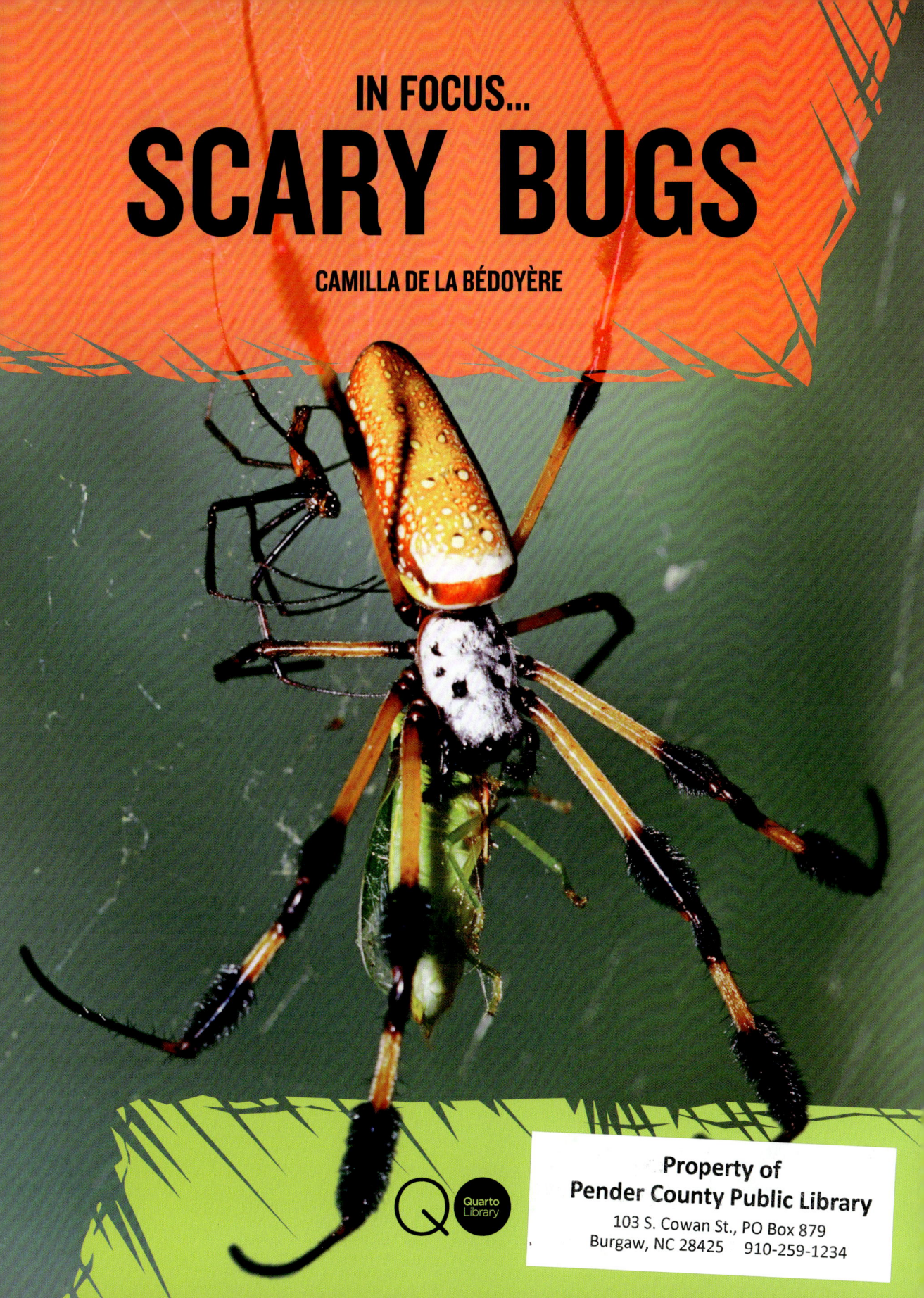

IN FOCUS...
SCARY BUGS

CAMILLA DE LA BÉDOYÈRE

Quarto is the authority on a wide range of topics.
Quarto educates, entertains and enriches the lives of our readers—enthusiasts and lovers of hands-on living.
www.quartoknows.com

This library edition published in 2019
by Quarto Library,
an imprint of The Quarto Group.
6 Orchard Road
Suite 100
Lake Forest, CA 92630
T: +1 949 380 7510
F: +1 949 380 7575
www.QuartoKnows.com

© 2019 Quarto Publishing plc

All rights reserved. No part of this publication may be reproduced, stored in a retrieval system, or transmitted in any form or by any means, electronic, mechanical, photocopying, recording, or otherwise, without the prior permission of the publisher, nor be otherwise circulated in any form of binding or cover other than that in which it is published and without a similar condition being imposed on the subsequent purchaser.

Distributed in the United States and Canada
by Lerner Publisher Services
241 First Avenue North
Minneapolis, MN 55401 U.S.A.
www.lernerbooks.com

A CIP record for this book is available from the Library of Congress.

ISBN 978 0 7112 4805 2

Manufactured in Guangdong, China CC072019

9 8 7 6 5 4 3 2 1

CONTENTS

*Words in **bold** are explained in the Glossary on page 31.*

INTRODUCTION 4
WOOD-EATING BEETLES 6
WASPS 8
WASPS' NESTS 10
ALL ABOUT ARACHNIDS 12
SPIDERS 14
TARANTULAS 16
SPITTING SPIDERS 18
ORB WEB SPIDERS 20
JUMPING SPIDERS 22
SCORPIONS 24
ATTACK AND DEFENSE..................... 26
BUG WORLD 28
GLOSSARY....................................... 31
INDEX... 32

INTRODUCTION

What makes a bug scary? Is it the eight dark eyes peering out from under a stone, or lots of hairy legs scuttling across the floor? Maybe it is the threat of venomous stings and acid bites that makes us fear some **insects** and their relatives.

FOUL FACT
Crab spiders vomit on their **prey** before eating it. The vomit turns the prey into liquid so the spider can suck it up!

Wandering spiders roam the jungle floor at night hunting for prey such as insects and frogs.

What are bugs?

Bugs and insects belong to a group of animals called arthropods. An arthropod's body is divided into parts called segments, which contain muscles and allow the animal's body to move. Arthropods have pairs of legs that bend at joints. Air moves into their body through gills, or through small holes in the exoskeleton.

Tiny terrors

Of course, bugs and insects are no scarier than any other group of animal—and most of them are so small that there is nothing to be frightened of. Some bugs are able to sting and bite people, and even spread diseases, but usually it's other bugs that have most to fear from these mini-monsters.

This Colorado beetle's stripes scare birds away. They warn predators that the beetle tastes bad.

Coconut crabs are crustaceans. One of these creepy arthropods can grow to more than 40 inches (1 meter) from leg-tip to leg-tip and weigh up to 10 pounds (4.5 kilograms)!

Big family

There are four main groups of arthropod: crustaceans, centipedes and millipedes, **arachnids**—which includes spiders—and insects. Of these, the insect group is the largest.

WOOD-EATING BEETLES

The **larvae** of many wood-eating beetles feed on dead and rotting trees. Others feed on live trees, furniture, and the wooden beams in houses.

Stag beetles

Male stag beetles have enormous jaws that look like the antlers of a stag deer. Like stags, they fight each other over females. Females lay their eggs in logs or dead tree stumps, and the larvae feed on juices from the rotting wood. The adults mostly feed on tree sap.

When stag beetles fight, the beetle with the largest jaws usually wins.

FOUL FACT
It can take a stag beetle larva five years of munching on rotten wood before it becomes a full-grown adult.

Longhorn beetle

Some wood-eaters, such as longhorn beetles, cause a lot of damage and are a serious pest. They lay their eggs in trees, and the larvae tunnel into the wood.

Longhorn beetles use their long antennae to feel what is in front, around, and behind them.

Deathwatch beetle

The deathwatch beetle bangs its head against wood to attract a **mate**. People used to think the tapping sound was a warning of death, because they often heard it in a hushed room where a person was dying. The female lays her eggs in the wood, and the larvae tunnel into it as they feed.

A deathwatch beetle chews its way in and out of wood, leaving behind holes and piles of sawdust.

WASPS

Wasps sometimes seem annoying to humans, but they're actually very useful. They feed their young on insects, such as caterpillars and **aphids**, which can damage plants.

FOUL FACT
In Japan, people die every year from the sting of the Asian giant hornet, which measures 2 inches (50 millimeters) long.

Adult wasps have strong jaws for biting into soft, sweet fruit.

European hornet

This large insect measures up to 1.25 inches (3 cm) long. It lives in colonies, in a nest built from a papery material that it makes by chewing up plants. The nest is usually in a tree or old building. The larvae eat insects caught by the adults.

A European hornet adult feeds on a bee that it has caught.

Spider wasps

The female spider wasp catches spiders to feed her young. She **paralyzes** the spider with her sting, and places her prey in a section of her nest with an egg. She then seals the section with mud. When the wasp larva hatches, it eats the spider.

The spider is still alive when the spider wasp seals it in her nest for the larvae to eat.

Yellow jackets

Common wasps are also known as yellow jackets. Like most wasps, they have a sting at the end of their body. This is shaped like a pointed tube, and is joined to a bag full of poison, or **venom**. The wasp uses its sting to attack prey and protect itself from enemies, including humans. After stinging, it can pull its sting out and use it again.

WASPS' NESTS

Wasps are some of the most skilled builders in the insect world. Some make their own nest, where they lay eggs and store food for their young. Others work together in big groups, or colonies, to build a large nest from mud or chewed wood pulp.

A female potter wasp carries a caterpillar back to her mud nest, to provide a food store for her young.

The papery material used to make the nest is waterproof.

Paper wasps

The paper wasp starts its nest alone. A female makes a few papery pockets from chewed up wood, mixed with her own spit. She then lays an egg in each pocket. Once her young are fully grown, they become **workers**, and she becomes the **queen**.  The workers make the nest bigger and the queen lays more eggs. In the fall, most wasps in the **colony** die, leaving behind one young queen.

Mud nests

Potter wasps live on their own. The female uses mud and water to build a nest that is shaped like a pot. She places her eggs and some food inside, and then closes the nest. The wasp larva break out of the nest when they become adults.

FOUL FACT
The queen is the only wasp in a colony that lives through the winter. She **hibernates**, then starts a new colony in the spring.

Parasol wasps fan their wings to keep the larvae cool

Parasol wasps

These wasps build an open, fan-shaped nest underneath tree branches. During the day, the wasps cluster underneath to protect their young. At night, they hunt for food to feed the growing larvae.

ALL ABOUT ARACHNIDS

Spiders and their relatives, such as scorpions and **mites**, are not insects. They belong to a separate family, called arachnids (say "uh-rack-nids.") Arachnids have four pairs of legs and do not have wings or antennae. There are at least 95,000 **species**, and they can be found all over the world.

The front section of a spider is protected by a tough plate called a carapace (say "ka-ruh-pace.")

Some species of scorpion have a sting that can be fatal to humans.

Scorpions

Scorpions are best-known for the dangerous sting at the end of their tail. When a scorpion attacks its prey, it swings its tail section forward over its body, so that it can drive the sting down into its victim.

FOUL FACT
The female black widow spider is bigger than the male. She often eats the male after **mating**!

A spider's body
Most spider bodies are split into two parts. The head and **thorax** are fused together to make one section. This is joined to the **abdomen** by a narrow waist. Most spiders have eight eyes and four pairs of legs. They also have silk-making organs, called **spinnerets**, in the abdomen.

Abdomen

Leg

Cephalothorax (say "sef-uh-low-thor-ax," head and thorax fused together)

This tiny mite lives in soil and feeds on other small insects.

Mites and ticks
Mites and ticks are tiny, but they occur in huge numbers. Some mites feed on plants, and others live as **parasites** on animals. Ticks feed on the blood of other animals, and are known to spread some dangerous diseases.

SPIDERS

There are at least 40,000 known species of spider, and many more that have not yet been named.

Life cycle

A female spider lays her eggs and protects them with an egg sac made from silk. Some spiders leave their egg sacs on plants. Others place them on a web or carry them around.

Deadly bite

When a spider bites its prey, poison flows through its **fangs** and freezes its victim, so it can't move. The poison dissolves the victim's insides, turning it into a liquid that the spider can suck up.

The strong jaws of a spider are armed with two large, curved fangs.

FOUL FACT

Nearly all spiders have a poisonous, or venomous, bite, but only a few are dangerous to humans.

Eyes

Most spiders have four pairs of eyes. The pattern in which they are arranged varies from one family to another. The pair at the front forms the images, and in many spiders the other eyes detect light. Jumping spiders have the best eyesight.

A jumping spider can swivel its large eyes.

Newly hatched spiders are called spiderlings. These ones have just left their egg sac.

TARANTULAS

Tarantulas are some of the largest of all spiders. Most hide during the day and come out at night to hunt insects and small creatures, which they kill with a poisonous bite.

Trapdoor spiders

These spiders have an unusual way of catching prey. The spider uses a mixture of mud, spit, and silk to make a burrow with a hinged lid. It then sits inside the burrow and waits for prey. As soon as it feels something moving past the lid, it jumps out, grabs the prey, and takes it back inside its burrow to eat.

Foul Fact
Female tarantulas can live to be 30 or 40 years old! The males have much shorter lives of about 10 years.

This trapdoor spider in Spain has pushed open the lid of its burrow and is about to pounce.

Goliath bird-eating spider

The Goliath bird-eating spider is the biggest spider in the world. It has a legspan of 12 inches (30 centimeters)! The spider does sometimes eat young birds, but mostly feeds on insects, mice, snakes, frogs, and lizards.

The Goliath bird eating spider lives in tropical rainforest in South America.

Females of this funnel web tarantula from Bolivia are twice the size of the males.

Funnel-web tarantulas

Spiders in this family make a messy, funnel-shaped web that leads into a burrow. If a frog, lizard, or insect walks across the web, the spider rushes out to kill it.

SPITTING SPIDERS

Some spiders spin webs to catch prey, and others spin them to protect their young. Some do not spin webs at all.

A female nursery web spider stands guard over her newly hatched spiderlings.

Nursery web spiders

The female nursery web spider makes a web to protect her young. She uses her jaws to carry her egg sac until the eggs are almost ready to hatch. Then she spins a web over the egg sac to keep it safe while the spiderlings crawl out.

Spitting spiders

These spiders trap their prey by spitting strings of sticky liquid over them. As they move toward their prey, they turn their head from side to side so the sticky strings criss-cross over the victim's body.

FOUL FACT

Young spiders use long strands of silk as parachutes to help them travel to new places. This is called ballooning.

A spitting spider sucks out the insides of its prey, which it has trapped with sticky strings.

Sheet-web weavers

These small spiders are sometimes called money spiders. They spin large, flat webs up to 12 inches (30 centimeters) wide. Lots of extra threads hold the web in place. When a flying insect hits one of these threads, it falls down onto the sheet web, where the spider is waiting.

This sheet-web weaver is eating a beetle it has caught in its web.

ORB WEB SPIDERS

Orb web spiders are some of the best known of all spiders. They make the webs that we often see in parks and gardens.

FOUL FACT

As soon as prey is caught in an orb-weaver's web, the spider rushes over and wraps it in silk to stop it from escaping.

An orb-weaver starts its web by making a non-sticky framework. Then it adds spokes and finally a sticky spiral for catching prey.

Garden orb-weaver

Like other orb-weavers, garden orb-weavers spin two types of silk. One type hardens into a tough, non-sticky thread and is used to strengthen the web. The other is sticky and is used to catch prey.

A small, male golden silk spider waits until the larger female is distracted before creeping up on her to mate.

Water spider

The water spider spins a bell-shaped home from silk and attaches it to a water plant. Then it fills the bell with bubbles of air that it collects at the surface. It waits inside the bell for prey to come near, pounces, and drags the prey back inside the bell to eat.

The water spider is the only spider that spends its whole life under water.

Golden silk spider

The female golden silk spider is eight or nine times the size of the male, and may weigh 100 times more than him. Like tiny insects that fly into her web, the male is too small to be worth attacking when he comes near her to try to mate with her.

JUMPING SPIDERS

Silk thread

FOUL FACT
Some jumping spiders can leap up to 50 times their own length.

Some spiders, such as jumping spiders and lynx spiders, have good eyesight and watch out for prey. Others rely more on their sense of touch. They sense movement through tiny hairs on their body and legs.

A giant crab spider flattens itself against a tree trunk to avoid being seen by a predator.

Giant crab spiders

These large spiders, also known as huntsman spiders or wood spiders, can be amazingly well **camouflaged**. They usually hunt at night for cockroaches and other insects.

Lynx spiders

Lynx spiders have long legs and run fast over plants to catch their prey, jumping from leaf to leaf. They have good eyesight, which helps them to spot their prey. Females usually guard their eggs until they hatch.

A green lynx spider in Costa Rica makes a dash for a plant bug.

A jumping spider leaps onto its fly prey (below), trailing a silk safety line.

Jumping spiders

Unlike many spiders, jumping spiders have good eyesight, and this helps them to find prey. Once they have spotted a victim, they pounce on it. However, before jumping, they fix a silk thread to the ground, so they can return along it safely to their hideout.

SCORPIONS

Most scorpions live in warm parts of the world. They use the poisonous sting at the end of their body to kill prey and protect themselves. Although scorpions have eyes, they cannot see well and find prey by using their sense of touch.

A female buthid scorpion carries her newly hatched young on her back until they can look after themselves.

Buthid scorpions

These large scorpions hide under stones during the day and come out at night to hunt. They grab insects and spiders in their powerful claws, or pincers. Then they swing their sting forward over their body and stab the victim.

Wind scorpions

Wind scorpions, also known as sun scorpions, are common in deserts. These fast-running hunters come out at night to prey on insects or small lizards. They can grow up to 6 inches (15 cm) long, not including the legs.

A wind scorpion's large jaws can cut through skin and thin bones.

FOUL FACT
Most other types of arachnid lay eggs, but scorpions give birth to live babies, known as scorplings.

Harvestmen

Sometimes known as daddy-long-legs, these arachnids have a round body and very long, thin legs. If they feel threatened, harvestmen may spray a bad-smelling liquid at their attacker.

Harvestmen usually come out at night to hunt for insects.

25

ATTACK AND DEFENSE

Insects have developed many different ways to protect themselves from predators. Lots of insects are also hunters. Some of them rely on speed or strength to catch their prey, and others use tricks and traps.

FOUL FACT

Stick insects can break off a leg to help them escape from a predator. If they're young, the leg will grow back!

The bright colors on this saddleback caterpillar warn enemies that it is poisonous.

Spikes and bright colors

Some types of caterpillars have spiky bodies to discourage attackers. Poisonous caterpillars are often brightly colored, which warns enemies to stay away.

The false eyes on this moth's wings have white centers, which makes them look even more like real eyes.

False eyes

Some insects make themselves look bigger than they really are. They have large markings on their wings that look like eyes. The eye spots trick predators into thinking they've seen a much bigger creature that would be difficult to catch.

These army ants are working together to attack a millipede, which they will feed to their colony.

Strength in numbers

Some insects, such as ants, hunt in groups. Working together, they can catch much larger prey than they would be able to on their own. They swarm all over a victim, such as a millipede or scorpion, and kill it with their bites.

BUG WORLD

It's a bug-eat-bug world! Although many small creatures look creepy, very few of them are a danger to humans. Most bugs use their skills of speed, stinging, stabbing, and biting to defend themselves, or to kill their prey.

Watching bugs

The world of bugs and insects is fascinating and fun to learn about. One of the best ways to discover how they live is to watch them from a safe distance. Look carefully for bugs that are camouflaged, or insects that use stripes or colors to warn that they have stings.

Bug hotels are stacks of wood, sticks, and pine cones that are full of small spaces where bugs can make a home.

Finding bugs

Bugs and insects are easiest to find on plants, under stones, and in the soil. Many of them live in ponds—you can look for them, with an adult's help, by pond-dipping. Take care as some bugs and insects can sting or bite, and keep them in separate pots so they don't kill one another! Always put them back where you found them, and wash your hands after touching bugs.

Pond-dipping is often organized at wildlife centers and parks. Pond water contains many small animals, especially insect larvae.

Saving bugs

Insects and bugs are food for bigger animals, they help plants to grow and they get rid of waste by recycling dead animals and plants. You can help protect their future by taking care of the environment. Recycling and reducing waste are simple ways we can all help to protect the natural world.

Plastic in the environment does great harm to living things. Reduce the amount of plastic you use, and always dispose of it properly and safely.

PICTURE CREDITS

BC = back cover, FC = front cover, b = bottom, c = center, t = top, l = left, r = right.

Alamy: 4cl Morley Read; 4-5 Gary Roberts; 5cr Panther Media GmbH; 9tl blickwinkel, 10-11 FLPA/Alamy Stock Photo; 22-23 F1online digitale Bildagentur GmbH; 27bl adrian hepworth; 30 F1online digitale Bildagentur GmbH

FLPA (www.flpa.co.uk) and its associate agencies: 1 Photo Researchers; 2 Claus Meyer/Minden Pictures; 6-7 Cyril Ruoso/Minden Pictures; 7tr Piotr Naskrecki/Minden Pictures; 7bl Mike Amphlett; 8-9 Matt Cole; 9cr Richard Becker; 10bl Alfred & Annaliese T/Imagebroker; 11bc Pete Oxford/Minden Pictures; 12l Frans Lanting; 12-13 ImageBroker/Imagebroker; 13c Nigel Cattlin; 14bl Emanuele Biggi; 16-17 Pete Oxford/Minden Pictures; 18bl Roger Tidman; 18-19 Piotr Naskrecki/Minden Pictures; 20bl FLPA; 20-21 Photo Researchers; 21r Eiichi Shinkai/Minden Pictures; 22bl Thomas Marent/Minden Pictures; 23tr Michael & Patricia Fogden/Minden Pictures; 24-25 Claus Meyer/Minden Pictures; 25tl Mark Moffett/Minden Pictures; 26-27 Rolf Nussbaumer/Imagebroker; 27t Cyril Ruoso/Minden Pictures

Getty Images: 15br Javier Aznar; 28-29 Ricky John Molloy

Nature Picture Library: 14-15 Bernard Castelein, 16b Hans Christoph Kappel; 19br Alex Hyde

Other: 17r Fritz Geller-Grimm

Shutterstock.com
FC Milan Zygmunt; BC By Milan Zygmunt; 25br Joseph Scott Photography; 28br Marjan Cermelj; 29bl Larina Marina

GLOSSARY

abdomen
back end of an insect's body, attached to the thorax

antennae
two long, thin feelers on an insect's head used to smell, taste, and touch things

aphids
tiny insects that feed by sucking sugary nectar from plants

arachnids
creatures with a 2-part body and 8 jointed legs. Spiders, scorpions, ticks, and mites are arachnids

camouflage
the colors or patterns on an animal's body that help it to blend in with its surroundings

colony
a group of insects of the same species living together in one place. Ants, termites, and some bees and wasps live in colonies.

fangs
sharp, pointed mouthparts, used to inject venom

hibernates
spends the winter sleeping to save energy

insects
animals with a head, thorax, abdomen, 3 pairs of legs, and 1 or 2 pairs of wings

larva/larvae
an insect's young, after it has hatched from an egg and before it becomes an adult

mate
one of a pair of animals that has chosen another to produce young.

mating
the coming together of male and female creatures to produce young

mites
tiny creatures related to spiders and ticks

paralyzes
makes it impossible for a creature to move all or part of its body

parasites
animals or plants that live on other animals or plants. Parasites often harm the thing they live on

predators
animals that hunt and kill other animals for food

prey
an animal that is hunted and eaten by another animal

queen
an egg-laying female in a colony of ants, bees, wasps, or termites

species
a group of animals with similar characteristics. Animals of the same species can mate and produce young

spinnerets
fine tubes at the end of a spider's abdomen. Silk for spinning a web comes out of the spider's body through the spinnerets.

thorax
the part of an insect's body between the head and the abdomen. An insect's legs are attached to the thorax

venom
A poisonous liquid used to kill or paralyze prey

workers
the insects in a colony that build the nest, find food, and care for young

INDEX

abdomen 13, 31
antennae 7, 12, 31
ants 27, 31
aphids 8, 31
arachnids 5, 12-13, 25, 31
army ants 27
arthropods 4-5
Asian giant hornets 8

bad-smelling liquid, spraying 25
ballooning 19
bees 9, 31
beetles 5, 6–7
bites 4, 5,14, 15, 16, 27, 29
black widow spiders 13
blood suckers 13
body parts 4, 13
buthid scorpions 24

camouflage 22, 28, 31
carapace 12
caterpillars 8, 10, 26
centipedes 5
cephalothorax 13
cockroaches 23
colonies 9, 10, 11, 27, 31
Colorado beetles 5
crab spiders 4
crustaceans 4, 5

daddy-long-legs 25
deathwatch beetles 7
diseases 5, 13

eggs 6, 7, 9, 10, 11, 14, 18, 23, 25
egg sacs 14, 18
European hornets 9
eyes 4, 13, 15, 24, 27
eye spots 27

fangs 14, 31
funnel-web tarantulas 17

garden orb-weavers 20
giant crab spiders 22
golden silk spiders 21
Goliath bird-eating spiders 17
green lynx spider 23

harvestmen 25
hibernation 11, 31
hornets 8, 9
huntsman spiders 22

jaws 6, 8, 14, 18, 25
jumping spiders 15, 22–23

larvae (see also caterpillars) 6, 7, 9, 11, 29, 31
longhorn beetles 7
lynx spiders 22, 23

mating 13, 31
millipedes 5, 27
mites 12, 13, 31
money spiders 19
moths 27

nests 9, 10-11, 31
nursery web spiders 18

orb-weaver spiders 20-21
orb web spiders 20-21

paper wasps 10
parasites 13, 31
parasol wasps 11
pests 7
pincers 24
potter wasps 10, 11

queen wasps 10, 11, 31

recycling 29

saddleback caterpillars 26
scorpions 12, 24-25, 27, 31
scorplings 25
sheet-web spiders 19
spiderlings 15, 18
spiders 4, 5, 9, 12-23, 31
spider wasps 9
spinnerets 13, 31
spitting spiders 18-19
stag beetles 6
stick insects 26
stings 4, 5, 8, 9, 12, 24, 28, 29
sun scorpions 25
swarms 27

tarantulas 16-17
termites 31
thorax 13, 31
ticks 13, 31
trapdoor spiders 16

venom/venomous 4, 9, 14, 15, 31

wandering spider 4
wasps 8-11, 31
water spiders 21
webs 14, 17, 18, 19, 20, 21, 31
wind scorpions 25
wood-eating beetles 6-7
wood spiders 22
workers 10, 31

yellow jackets 9